소나기

아시아에서는 《바이링궐 에디션 한국 대표 소설》을 기획하여 한국의 우수한 문학을 주제별로 엄선해 국내외 독자들에게 소개합니다. 이 기획은 국내외 우수한 번역가들이 참여하여 원작의 품격을 최대한 살렸습니다. 문학을 통해 아시아의 정체성과 가치를 살피는 데 주력해 온 아시아는 한국인의 삶을 넓고 깊게 이해하는 데 이 기획이 기여하기를 기대합니다.

Asia Publishers presents some of the very best modern Korean literature to readers worldwide through its new Korean literature series 〈Bilingual Edition Modern Korean Literature〉. We are proud and happy to offer it in the most authoritative translation by renowned translators of Korean literature. We hope that this series helps to build solid bridges between citizens of the world and Koreans through a rich in-depth understanding of Korea.

바이링궐 에디션 한국 대표 소설 106

Bi-lingual Edition Modern Korean Literature 106

The Cloudburst

황순원
소나기

Hwang Sun-Won

ASIA
PUBLISHERS

Contents

소나기

The Cloudburst

소년은 개울가에서 소녀를 보자 곧 윤초시네 증손녀딸이라는 걸 알 수 있었다. 소녀는 개울에다 손을 잠그고 물장난을 하고 있는 것이다. 서울서는 이런 개울물을 보지 못하기나 한 듯이.

벌써 며칠째 소녀는 학교서 돌아오는 길에 물장난이었다. 그런데 어제까지는 개울 기슭에서 하더니 오늘은 징검다리 한가운데 앉아서 하고 있다.

소년은 개울둑에 앉아버렸다. 소녀가 비키기를 기다리자는 것이다.

요행 지나가는 사람이 있어 소녀가 길을 비켜주었다.

When the boy first saw the girl by the stream, he knew right away she must be the Yun's great-granddaughter. She was dipping her hand in the stream and splashing the water. As if this stream was something you don't see in Seoul.

The girl had been stopping by the stream like this for several days on her way home from school. Yesterday she had stayed at the edge of the stream, but today she was sitting right in the middle of the stepping-stones.

The boy sat down on the dike beside the stream. He thought he would watch until the girl had to move aside to let someone pass.

다음날은 좀 늦게 개울가로 나왔다.

이날은 소녀가 징검다리 한가운데 앉아 세수를 하고 있었다. 분홍 스웨터 소매를 걷어 올린 팔과 목덜미가 마냥 희었다.

한참 세수를 하고 나더니 이번에는 물속을 빤히 들여다본다. 얼굴이라도 비추어보는 것이리라. 갑자기 물을 움켜낸다. 고기 새끼라도 지나가는 듯.

소녀는 소년이 개울둑에 앉아 있는 걸 아는지 모르는지 그냥 날쌔게 물만 움켜낸다. 그러나 번번이 허탕이다. 그래도 재미있는 양, 자꾸 물만 움킨다. 어제처럼 개울을 건너는 사람이 있어야 길을 비킬 모양이다.

그러다가 소녀가 물속에서 무엇을 하나 집어낸다. 하얀 조약돌이었다. 그러고는 훌 일어나 팔짝팔짝 징검다리를 뛰어 건너간다.

다 건너가더니 홱 이리로 돌아서며,

"이 바보."

조약돌이 날아왔다.

소년은 저도 모르게 벌떡 일어섰다.

단발머리를 나풀거리며 소녀가 막 달린다. 갈밭 사잇길로 들어섰다. 뒤에는 청량한 가을 햇살 아래 빛나는

It happened that someone did come along, and the girl moved away to let the person cross.

The next day he went to the stream a little later. This time the girl was washing her face and hands as she sat at the middle of the stepping-stones. She had pushed up the sleeves of her pink sweater, and her arms and neck looked especially fair.

After she had washed for quite a while, she looked intently at the water. Probably she was looking at the reflection of her face. Suddenly she thrust her hand into the water, as though she was trying to catch a little fish passing.

Without any sign that she knew the boy was sitting on the dike, the girl kept splashing the water nimbly with her hands. But as always, she caught nothing. She enjoyed it all the same, though, as she kept catching handfuls of water. It looked as if someone would have to come and cross the stream or she would never move.

After a while the girl took something out of the water. It was a small white stone. She jumped up and ran springing over the stones to the other side.

As soon as she was all the way across, she spun around, and facing the stream she said, "Dummy!"

갈꽃뿐.

이제 저쯤 갈밭머리로 소녀가 나타나리라. 꽤 오랜 시간이 지났다고 생각했다. 그런데도 소녀는 나타나지 않는다. 발돋움을 했다. 그러고도 상당한 시간이 지났다고 생각됐다.

저쪽 갈밭머리에 갈꽃이 한 옴큼 움직였다. 소녀가 갈꽃을 안고 있었다. 그리고 이제는 천천한 걸음이었다. 유난히 맑은 가을 햇살이 소녀의 갈꽃머리에서 반짝거렸다. 소녀 아닌 갈꽃이 들길을 걸어가는 것만 같았다.

소년은 이 갈꽃이 아주 뵈지 않게 되기까지 그대로 서 있었다. 문득 소녀가 던진 조약돌을 내려다보았다. 물기가 걷혀 있었다. 소년은 조약돌을 집어 주머니에 넣었다.

다음날부터 좀 더 늦게 개울가로 나왔다. 소녀의 그림자가 뵈지 않았다. 다행이었다.

그러나 이상한 일이었다. 소녀의 그림자가 뵈지 않는 날이 계속될수록 소년의 가슴 한구석에는 어딘가 허전함이 자리잡는 것이었다. 주머니 속 조약돌을 주무르는 버릇이 생겼다.

The little stone flew through the air.

The boy stood right up without realizing what he was doing.

The girl ran hard, with her loose, short hair flying. She ran to the path between the reed fields. He could see only the shimmering reed tassels in the crisp autumn sunlight. Then it was time for the girl to appear at the far end of the reed fields. It seemed to him that a long time had already passed. Still the girl did not appear. He stood on tiptoe and looked again. And once more he thought a long time had gone by.

Over at the far end of the reed fields a few of the tassels moved. The girl was holding an armful of reeds. Now she was walking slowly. The crystal clear autumn sunlight glistened on the heads of the reeds the girl was carrying. It looked as if the armful of reeds was walking by itself.

The boy stood where he was until the tassels had completely disappeared from view. Suddenly he looked down and saw the little stone the girl had thrown. He picked it up and put it in his pocket.

From the next day on the boy went down to the stream a little later in the day. No trace of the girl

그러한 어떤 날, 소년은 전에 소녀가 앉아 물장난을 하던 징검다리 한가운데에 앉아 보았다. 물속에 손을 잠갔다. 세수를 하였다. 물속을 들여다보았다. 검게 탄 얼굴이 그대로 비치었다. 싫었다.

소년은 두 손으로 물속의 얼굴을 움키었다. 몇 번이고 움키었다. 그러다가 깜짝 놀라 일어나고 말았다. 소녀가 이리 건너오고 있지 않으냐.

숨어서 내 하는 꼴을 엿보고 있었구나. 소년은 달리기 시작했다. 디딤돌을 헛짚었다. 한 발이 물속에 빠졌다. 더 달렸다.

몸을 가릴 데가 있어줬으면 좋겠다. 이쪽 길에는 갈밭도 없다. 메밀밭이다. 전에 없이 메밀꽃내가 짜릿하니 코를 찌른다고 생각됐다. 미간이 아찔했다. 찝찔한 액체가 입술에 흘러들었다. 코피였다. 소년은 한 손으로 코피를 훔쳐내면서 그냥 달렸다. 어디선가, 바보, 바보, 하는 소리가 자꾸만 뒤따라오는 것 같았다.

토요일이었다.

개울가에 이르니 며칠째 보이지 않던 소녀가 건너편 가에 앉아 물장난을 하고 있었다.

was to be seen. That was lucky.

But a strange thing happened. The more days that went by without a glimpse of the girl, the more the boy began to feel a vague emptiness somewhere in a corner of his heart. He found that he was in the habit of fingering the little stone in his pocket.

One day the boy went and tried sitting in the middle of the stepping-stones where the girl had sat and splashed her hands in the water. He put his hand in the water. He washed his face and hands. He looked down at the water. The surface faithfully reflected his dark, tanned face. He didn't want to look at it.

The boy churned the face in the water with both hands. He repeated this several times. Then suddenly he started and stood straight up. Wasn't that the girl coming his way?

"She was hiding and watching what I was doing!" The boy began to run. He slipped on one of the stepping-stones. One foot went in the water. He kept running.

If only he could find a place to hide from her. Along this path there were no reeds, only buckwheat. The fragrance of the buckwheat in bloom was more overpowering than he had ever known it

모르는 체 징검다리를 건너기 시작했다. 얼마 전에 소녀 앞에서 한 번 실수를 했을 뿐, 여태 큰길 가듯이 건너던 징검다리를 오늘은 조심성스럽게 건넌다.

"얘."

못 들은 체했다. 둑 위로 올라섰다.

"얘, 이게 무슨 조개지?"

자기도 모르게 돌아섰다. 소녀의 맑고 검은 눈과 마주쳤다. 얼른 소녀의 손바닥으로 눈을 떨구었다.

"비단조개."

"이름두 참 곱다."

갈림길에 왔다. 여기서 소녀는 아래편으로 한 삼 마장쯤, 소년은 우대로 한 십 리 가까잇길을 가야 한다.

소녀가 걸음을 멈추며,

"너 저 산 너머에 가본 일 있니?"

벌 끝을 가리켰다.

"없다."

"우리 가보지 않을래? 시골 오니까 혼자서 심심해 못 견디겠다."

"저래봬두 멀다."

"멀믄 얼마나 멀갔게? 서울 있을 땐 아주 먼 데까지

could be. He thought his nose would burst. He began to feel dizzy. A salty liquid ran onto his lips. His nose was bleeding.

He wiped away the blood with one hand and kept running. It seemed as though he could hear "Dummy! Dummy!" following him as he ran.

It was a Saturday. He had not seen the girl for several days, but when he arrived at the stream, she was sitting on the opposite bank splashing in the water.

He began to cross on the stepping-stones, pretending not to notice her. He was used to walking on these stones as if they were a wide road, but today he stepped cautiously, even though the slip he had made in front of her the last time had only been a slight misstep.

"Hey!"

The boy pretended not to hear. He went up and stood on the dike.

"Hey, what kind of shell is this?"

Without thinking he turned around. He found himself looking into her clear, black eyes. Immediately he dropped his gaze to the girl's palm.

"Satin shell."

소풍 갔었다."

소녀의 눈이 금세, 바보, 바보, 할 것만 같았다.

논 사잇길로 들어섰다. 벼 가을걷이하는 곁을 지났다.

허수아비가 서 있었다. 소년이 새끼줄을 흔들었다. 참새가 몇 마리 날아간다. 참 오늘은 일찍 집으로 돌아가 텃논의 참새를 봐야 할걸 하는 생각이 든다.

"아, 재밌다!"

소녀가 허수아비 줄을 잡더니 흔들어댄다. 허수아비가 대고 우쭐거리며 춤을 춘다. 소녀의 왼쪽 볼에 살포시 보조개가 패었다.

저만치 허수아비가 또 서 있다. 소녀가 그리로 달려간다. 그 뒤를 소년도 달렸다. 오늘 같은 날은 일찌감치 집으로 돌아가 집안일을 도와야 한다는 생각을 잊어버리기라도 하려는 듯이.

소녀의 곁을 스쳐 그냥 달린다. 메뚜기가 따끔따끔 얼굴에 와 부딪친다. 쪽빛으로 한껏 갠 가을 하늘이 소년의 눈앞에서 맴을 돈다. 어지럽다. 저놈의 독수리, 저놈의 독수리, 저놈의 독수리가 맴을 돌고 있기 때문이다.

돌아다보니 소녀는 지금 자기가 지나쳐온 허수아비를 흔들고 있다. 좀 전 허수아비보다 더 우쭐거린다.

"Even the name is pretty."

They came to the fork in the road. Here the girl had a few hundred yards to go by the lower road, while the boy would travel two or three miles on the upper road.

Pausing here, the girl pointed to the far edge of a field and asked, "Have you ever been to the other side of that hill?"

"No."

"Don't you think we should go and look? Here in the country I'm so bored I don't know what I'm going to do!"

"It's pretty far to go."

"That depends on what you mean by 'far.' When I was in Seoul I used to go really far on picnics." When she said that, the girl's eyes seemed to be saying, "Dummy! Dummy!"

They came to a raised path between the rice paddies. They passed people harvesting early rice.

They found a scarecrow. The boy shook the straw ropes holding it up. Some sparrows flew away. He thought, "Oh, I really ought to go home early today and keep the sparrows out of the field next to the house."

"Oh, what fun!" The girl took hold of the lines on

논이 끝난 곳에 도랑이 하나 있었다. 소녀가 먼저 뛰어 건넜다.

거기서부터 산 밑까지는 밭이었다.

수숫단을 세워 놓은 밭머리를 지났다.

"저게 뭐니?"

"원두막."

"여기 차미, 맛있니?"

"그럼. 차미맛두 좋지만 수박맛은 더 좋다."

"하나 먹어봤으면."

소년이 참외그루에 심은 무밭으로 들어가, 무 두 밑을 뽑아왔다. 아직 밑이 덜 들어 있었다. 잎을 비틀어 팽개친 후 소녀에게 한 밑 건넨다. 그러고는 이렇게 먹어야 한다는 듯이 먼저 대강이를 한 입 베물어낸 다음 손톱으로 한 돌이 껍질을 벗겨 우적 깨문다.

소녀도 따라 했다. 그러나 세 입도 못 먹고,

"아, 맵고 지려."

하며 집어던지고 만다.

"참 맛없어 못 먹겠다."

소년이 더 멀리 팽개쳐버렸다.

the scarecrow and shook them. The scarecrow swayed and danced. The dimples were softly outlined on the girl's left cheek.

A little farther on stood another scarecrow. The girl ran over to it. The boy ran behind her, as if trying to forget that on a day like this he ought to go home early and help with the chores.

He brushed past the girl and kept running. The grasshoppers flying against him made his face sting. The autumn sky, a deep indigo, spun before the boy's eyes. He was dizzy. It was because of that eagle, that eagle, that eagle circling up there in the sky.

He looked back and saw the girl shaking a scarecrow. It was dancing even more than the first one.

At the end of the rice paddies they came to a ditch. The girl ran there first and jumped across. From there to the base of the hill there were only a few farm fields.

They passed some sorghum fields where harvested shocks were standing.

"What's that?"

"A watchman's hut."

"Are the melons here good?"

"Sure, the melons are good, but the watermelons

산이 가까워졌다.

단풍이 눈에 따가웠다.

"야아!"

소녀가 산을 향해 달려갔다. 이번은 소년이 뒤따라 달리지 않았다. 그러고도 곧 소녀보다 더 많은 꽃을 꺾었다.

"이게 들국화, 이게 싸리꽃, 이게 도라지꽃……."

"도라지꽃이 이렇게 예쁜 줄은 몰랐네. 난 보랏빛이 좋아! ……근데 이 양산같이 생긴 노란 꽃이 뭐지?"

"마타리꽃."

소녀는 마타리꽃을 양산 받듯이 해보인다. 약간 상기된 얼굴에 살폿한 보조개를 떠올리며.

다시 소년은 꽃 한 옴큼을 꺾어왔다. 싱싱한 꽃가지만 골라 소녀에게 건넨다.

그러나 소녀는,

"하나두 버리지 말어."

산마루께로 올라갔다.

맞은편 골짜기에 오손도손 초가집이 몇 모여 있었다.

누가 말한 것도 아닌데 바위에 나란히 걸터앉았다. 별로[1] 주위가 조용해진 것 같았다. 따가운 가을 햇살만이

are even better."

"I wish I could eat one."

The boy went into a melon field that had been second cropped in radishes and pulled up two big daikon radishes. They weren't quite fully grown. After twisting off the leaves and throwing them down, he handed her one of the radishes. Then as if to show her how they were eaten, he bit off the top, scraped away a ring of the skin with his fingernail and began to crunch it.

The girl did the same. By the third bite, though, she said, "Oh, it's too hot, and it stinks!" She spat it out and threw the rest away.

"It tastes awful! I can't eat it."

He flung his radish even farther away.

The hill drew closer. The autumn leaves on the hill stood out vividly.

"Oh, look!" The girl ran in the direction of the hill. This time the boy did not run after her, but soon he had picked more flowers than she had.

"These are wild chrysanthemums, these are bush clover, these are bluebells."

"I didn't know bluebells were so pretty. I like purple anyway. Then what are those yellow flowers that look like parasols?"

말라가는 풀 냄새를 퍼뜨리고 있었다.

"저건 또 무슨 꽃이지?"

적잖이 비탈진 곳에 칡덩굴이 엉키어 끝물꽃을 달고 있었다.

"꼭 등꽃 같네. 서울 우리 학교에 큰 등나무가 있었단다. 저 꽃을 보니까 등나무 밑에서 놀던 동무들 생각이 난다."

소녀가 조용히 일어나 비탈진 곳으로 간다. 꽃송이가 달린 줄기를 잡고 끊기 시작한다. 좀처럼 끊어지지 않는다. 안간힘을 쓰다가 그만 미끄러지고 만다. 칡덩굴을 그러쥐었다.

소년이 놀라 달려갔다. 소녀가 손을 내밀었다. 손을 잡아 이끌어 올리며, 소년은 제가 꺾어다 줄 것을 잘못했다고 뉘우친다.

소녀의 오른쪽 무릎에 핏방울이 내맺혔다. 소년은 저도 모르게 생채기에 입술을 가져다대고 빨기 시작했다. 그러다가 무슨 생각을 했는지 홱 일어나 저쪽으로 달려간다.

좀만에 숨이 차 돌아온 소년은,

"이걸 바르면 낫는다."

"Wild parsley."

The girl held up a flower the way you would hold a parasol. This brought out the delicate dimples on the girl's slightly flushed face.

Once more the boy picked a handful of flowers and brought them over to the girl. He picked out the freshest among them and handed them to her. She said, "Don't throw any of them away."

They walked up the ridge to the crest of the hill. Over in the opposite valley several thatched farm-houses were gathered into a cozy little hamlet.

Neither suggested it, but they sat down side by side astride a big boulder. The surroundings seemed to become especially hushed. The autumn sunlight filled the air with the fragrance of drying grasses and leaves.

"What are those flowers over there?"

On a rather steep slope nearby flowers hung from a tangled arrowroot vine.

"They look like wisteria. There used to be a big wisteria arbor at our school in Seoul. When I see those flowers it makes me think of the times I used to spend with my friends under that wisteria arbor."

The girl rose slowly and went over to the slope. She backed down on her hands and knees, and

송진을 생채기에다 문질러 바르고는 그 달음으로 칡덩굴 있는 데로 내려가 꽃 달린 줄기를 이빨로 끊어가지고 올라온다. 그러고는,

"저기 송아지가 있다. 그리 가보자."

누렁송아지였다. 아직 코뚜레도 꿰지 않았다.

소년이 고삐를 바투 잡아 쥐고 등을 긁어주는 척 후딱 올라탔다. 송아지가 껑충거리며 돌아간다.

소녀의 흰 얼굴이, 분홍 스웨터가, 남색 스커트가, 안고 있는 꽃과 함께 범벅이 된다. 모두가 하나의 큰 꽃묶음 같다. 어지럽다. 그러나 내리지 않으리라. 자랑스러웠다. 이것만은 소녀가 흉내내지 못할 자기 혼자만이 할 수 있는 일인 것이다.

"너희 예서 뭣들 하느냐?"

농부 하나가 억새풀 사이로 올라왔다.

송아지 등에서 뛰어내렸다. 어린 송아지를 타서 허리가 상하면 어쩌느냐고 꾸지람을 들을 것만 같다.

그런데 나룻이 긴 농부는 소녀 편을 한번 흝어보고는 그저 송아지 고삐를 풀어내면서,

"어서들 집으루 가거라. 소나기가 올라."

참 먹장구름 한 장이 머리 위에 와 있다. 갑자기 사면

began to tug on the vine that had the most blossoms hanging from it. It hardly moved as she pulled. She tried to check herself, but began to slide. She held on to the arrowroot vine.

The boy jumped up and ran to her. The girl put out her hand, and as the boy pulled her up he thought that he should have offered to pick the flowers. Beads of blood began to form on the girl's right knee. Without thinking the boy put his lips on the scratch and began to suck away the blood. Then suddenly he thought of something, jumped up and ran off.

In a short while the boy returned out of breath and said, "If you rub this on, it'll get better."

The boy daubed some pine resin on the scratch, and then he went down to the place where the arrowroot vines were growing. With his teeth he tore off several of the vines with the most blossoms, and climbed back up with them. After this he said, "There's a calf over there. Let's go see it."

The calf was a light yellowish color. It still did not have the ring put through its nose.

The boy grasped the tether close to the calf's head, acted as if he were about to scratch its back, then lightly jumped up and mounted it. The calf

이 소란스러워진 것 같다. 바람이 우수수 소리를 내며 지나간다. 삽시간에 주위가 보랏빛으로 변했다.

산을 내려오는데 떡갈나무 잎에서 빗방울 듣는 소리가 난다. 굵은 빗방울이었다. 목덜미가 선뜻선뜻했다. 그러자 대번에 눈앞을 가로막는 빗줄기.

비안개 속에 원두막이 보였다. 그리로 가 비를 그을 수밖에.

그러나 원두막은 기둥이 기울고 지붕도 갈래갈래 찢어져 있었다. 그런대로 비가 덜 새는 곳을 가려 소녀를 들어서게 했다. 소녀는 입술이 파랗게 질려 있었다. 어깨를 자꾸 떨었다.

무명 겹저고리를 벗어 소녀의 어깨를 싸주었다. 소녀는 비에 젖은 눈을 들어 한번 쳐다보았을 뿐, 소년이 하는 대로 잠자코 있었다. 그러면서 안고 온 꽃묶음 속에서 가지가 꺾이고 꽃이 일그러진 송이를 골라 발밑에 버린다.

소녀가 들어선 곳도 비가 새기 시작했다. 더 거기서 비를 그을 수 없었다.

밖을 내다보던 소년이 무엇을 생각했는지 수수밭 쪽으로 달려간다. 세워 놓은 수숫단 속을 비집어 보더니

began to buck and circle.

The girl's white face, pink sweater, dark blue skirt, and the flowers she was holding in her arms all swirled into one blur. It looked like one great bunch of flowers. Oh, I'm dizzy! But he didn't want to get off. He was feeling proud of himself. Here was one thing he could do that the girl couldn't imitate, he thought.

"What's going on here?" A farmer appeared, coming up through the tall reeds.

The boy jumped down from the calf. Now all this would end up with a scolding, with farmer saying you ought to know you'll hurt the back of such a small calf if you try to ride it.

But the farmer, who had a long beard, glanced in the direction of the girl, untied the tether of the calf and said to them, "You'd better hurry home. It's about to rain."

Sure enough, a black storm cloud was directly overhead. All at once loud noise seemed to be coming from every direction. The wind rose and swooshed around. In a moment everything around them turned purple.

As they came down the hill they heard the sound of raindrops on the leaves of the oak trees. They

옆의 수숫단을 날라다 덧세운다. 다시 속을 비집어 본다. 그러고는 소녀 쪽을 향해 손짓을 한다.

수숫단 속은 비는 안 새었다. 그저 어둡고 좁은 게 안됐다. 앞에 나앉은 소년은 그냥 비를 맞아야만 했다. 그런 소년의 어깨에서 김이 올랐다.

소녀가 속삭이듯이, 이리 들어와 앉으라고 했다. 괜찮다고 했다. 소녀가 다시 들어와 앉으라고 했다. 할 수 없이 뒷걸음질을 쳤다. 그 바람에 소녀가 안고 있는 꽃묶음이 우그러들었다. 그러나 소녀는 상관없다고 생각했다. 비에 젖은 소년의 몸 내음새가 확 코에 끼얹혀졌다. 그러나 고개를 돌리지 않았다. 도리어 소년의 몸 기운으로 해서 떨리던 몸이 적이 누그러지는 느낌이었다.

소란하던 수숫잎 소리가 뚝 그쳤다. 밖이 멀개졌다.

수숫단 속을 벗어나왔다. 멀지 않은 앞쪽에 햇빛이 눈부시게 내리붓고 있었다.

도랑 있는 곳까지 와보니, 엄청나게 물이 불어 있었다. 빛마저 제법 붉은 흙탕물이었다. 뛰어 건널 수가 없었다.

소년이 등을 돌려댔다. 소녀가 순순히 업혔다. 걷어 올린 소년의 잠방이까지 물이 올라왔다. 소녀는, 어머

were big drops of rain. They felt the cold on the back of their necks. Then suddenly there was a cloudburst that at once blinded their view.

In the dense downpour they saw the little watchman's hut. It was the only place to take cover from the rain.

The stilts under the little hut were leaning askew and the thatched roof had separated in several places.

Such as it was, the boy found a spot where the rain was leaking in less badly and had the girl go inside and wait there.

The girl's lips began to turn a blotchy blue color, and her shoulders kept shaking and shaking.

The boy took off his cotton jacket and put it around the girl's shoulders. The girl raised her drenched eyes and looked at the boy. The boy stood there silently. Then she removed the flowers with broken stems and wilted blossoms from the bunch she had been carrying in her arms, and dropped them by her feet. The rain began to leak in where the girl was standing. It was impossible to stay out of the rain there any longer.

The boy looked outside, then thought of something and ran over toward the sorghum field. He

나 소리를 지르며 소년의 목을 그러안았다.

개울가에 다다르기 전에 가을 하늘은 언제 그랬는가 싶게 구름 한 점 없이 쪽빛으로 개어 있었다.

그다음날은 소녀의 모양이 뵈지 않았다. 다음날도, 다음날도. 매일같이 개울가로 달려와 봐도 뵈지 않았다.

학교에서 쉬는 시간에 운동장을 살피기도 했다. 남몰래 오학년 여자반을 엿보기도 했다. 그러나 뵈지 않았다.

그날도 소년은 주머니 속 흰 조약돌만 만지작거리며 개울가로 나왔다. 그랬더니 이쪽 개울둑에 소녀가 앉아 있는 게 아닌가.

소년은 가슴부터 두근거렸다.

"그동안 앓았다."

알아보게 소녀의 얼굴이 해쓱해져 있었다.

"그날 소나기 맞은 것 때메?"

소녀가 가만히 고개를 끄덕였다.

"인제 다 낫냐?"

"아직두……."

"그럼 누워 있어야지."

pulled open one of the tall sheaves standing in the field, then brought several more nearby sheaves and stood them against it. He looked inside once again, then looked toward the hut and beckoned.

The rain did not leak into the tall sorghum sheaves. But it was dark and the space was too small. The boy, sitting in front of the girl, was partly exposed to the rain. Vapor was now rising from the boy's shoulders.

In a near-whisper the girl said, "Come in and sit here."

"I'm all right."

She said once again, "Come in and sit down."

He had to back in. When he did, he crushed the bunch of flowers the girl was holding, but she did not seem to mind. The odor of the boy's rain-soaked body suddenly hit her nostrils, but she did not turn her head away. Instead she began to feel the vigor of the boy's body infuse her shivering frame with its warmth.

All at once the sound on the leaves of the sorghum shocks stopped. Outside it began to turn brighter.

They came out of their shelter in the tall shocks. Ahead on the path the blinding sunlight was already

"너무 갑갑해서 나왔다. ……그날 참 재밌었어. ……근데 그날 어디서 이런 물이 들었는지 잘 지지 않는다."

소녀가 분홍 스웨터 앞자락을 내려다본다. 거기에 검붉은 진흙물 같은 게 들어 있었다.

소녀가 가만히 보조개를 떠올리며,

"이게 무슨 물 같니?"

소년은 스웨터 앞자락만 바라다보고 있었다.

"내 생각해 냈다. 그날 도랑 건널 때 네게 업힌 일 있지? 그때 네 등에서 옮은 물이다."

소년은 얼굴이 확 달아오름을 느꼈다.

갈림길에서 소녀는,

"저 오늘 아침에 우리 집에서 대추를 땄다. 낼 제사 지내려구……."

대추 한 줌을 내어준다.

소년은 주춤한다.

"맛봐라, 우리 증조할아버지가 심었다는데 아주 달다."

소년은 두 손을 오그려 내밀며,

"참 알두 굵다!"

"그리구 저, 우리 이번에 제사 지내구 나서 좀 있다 집

pouring down. When they came to the place where they had crossed the ditch, they found it had swollen beyond recognition. The color had changed and it had turned into a rushing, muddy river. It would be impossible now to jump across.

The boy turned and offered his back. The girl calmly climbed onto his back to be carried across. The water came up over his rolled-up shorts. The girl cried out, "Oh my!" and held on tightly around the boy's neck. Before they had reached the opposite bank, the autumn sky had cleared and was in its glory as never before, a high deep-blue dome without a speck of cloud to be seen.

After that day the girl was nowhere to be seen. Every day the boy would run to the place by the side of the stream but could never find her.

The boy even watched the school playground during recess hours. He began to spy furtively on the girl's fifth grade class, but he did not see her.

Then one day as usual the boy went down to the bank of the stream, fingering the little white stone he still carried in his pocket. And look, wasn't that the girl sitting on the dike on this side of the stream?

을 내주게 됐다."

소년은 소녀네가 이사해 오기 전에 벌써 어른들의 이야기를 들어서 윤초시 손자가 서울서 사업에 실패해 가지고 고향에 돌아오지 않을 수 없게 됐다는 걸 알고 있었다. 그것이 이번에는 고향집마저 남의 손에 넘기게 된 모양이었다.

"왜 그런지 난 이사 가는 게 싫어졌다. 어른들이 하는 일이니 어쩔 수 없지만……."

전에 없이 소녀의 까만 눈에 쓸쓸한 빛이 떠돌았다.

소녀와 헤어져 돌아오는 길에 소년은 혼자 속으로 소녀가 이사를 간다는 말을 수없이 되뇌어 보았다. 무어 그리 안타까울 것도 서러울 것도 없었다. 그렇건만 소년은 지금 자기가 씹고 있는 대추알의 단맛을 모르고 있었다.

이날 밤, 소년은 몰래 덕쇠 할아버지네 호두밭으로 갔다.

낮에 봐두었던 나무로 올라갔다. 그리고 봐두었던 가지를 향해 작대기를 내리쳤다. 호두송이 떨어지는 소리가 별나게 크게 들렸다. 가슴이 선뜩했다. 그러나 다음 순간, 굵은 호두야 많이 떨어져라, 많이 떨어져라, 저도

The boy's heart began to thump.

"I've been sick since I saw you."

The girl's face seemed to have turned a much paler color.

"Is it because you were caught in the rain that day?"

She quietly nodded her head.

"Are you all better now?"

"Well, I'm still..." she trailed off and did not finish.

"Then you ought to be lying down and resting."

"I came out because I was so bored. Oh, that day was so much fun! You know, I got a stain on my clothes that won't come out."

The girl looked down at the bottom edge of her pink sweater. There was a dark, reddish stain there the color of muddy water.

Gently bringing to life her faint dimples, the girl said, "Where do you suppose this stain came from?"

The boy stood looking intently at the hem of the sweater.

"I think I know. Remember how you carried me on your back across the ditch that day? I picked up that stain from your back."

The boy felt himself suddenly blushing.

At the place where they took separate paths the girl said, "Say, this morning we picked dates at our

모를 힘에 이끌려 마구 작대기를 내리치는 것이었다.

돌아오는 길에는 열이틀 달이 지우는 그늘만 골라 짚었다. 그늘의 고마움을 처음 느꼈다.

불룩한 주머니를 어루만졌다. 호두송이를 맨손으로 깠다가는 옴이 오르기 쉽다는 말 같은 건 아무렇지도 않았다. 그저 근동에서 제일가는 이 덕쇠 할아버지네 호두를 어서 소녀에게 맛보여야 한다는 생각만이 앞섰다.

그러다, 아차, 하는 생각이 들었다. 소녀더러 병이 좀 낫거들랑 이사 가기 전에 한번 개울가로 나와 달라는 말을 못 해둔 것이었다. 바보 같은 것, 바보 같은 것.

이튿날, 소년이 학교에서 돌아오니 아버지가 나들이 옷으로 갈아입고 닭 한 마리를 안고 있었다.

어디 가시냐고 물었다.

그 말에는 대꾸도 없이 아버지는 안고 있는 닭의 무게를 겨냥해 보면서,

"이만하면 될까?"

어머니가 망태기를 내주며,

"벌써 며칠째 걀걀하구 알 날 자리를 보던데요. 크진

house. We're getting ready for the autumn sacrifice tomorrow."

She held out a handful of dates. The boy hesitated.

"Try them. They're very sweet. They say our great-great-grandfather planted the tree."

Extending his cupped hands, the boy said, "They sure are big."

"Oh, and by the way, after the autumn moon sacrifice, we're going to move out of our house."

Even before the girl and her family had moved in, the boy had heard the people in the village saying that Yun's grandson was coming back to the home village because the family had failed in business in Seoul and had no place else to go. Now it looked as if they had lost the family homestead, too.

"I don't know why, but now I don't want to move," the girl said. "The grownups have made the decision, so there isn't anything I can do about it, and yet..." and she fell silent.

For the first time a lonesome look came into the girl's black eyes.

On his way home after he had left the girl, the boy kept thinking over and over about the girl's saying

않아두 살은 쪘을 거예요."

소년이 이번에는 어머니한테 아버지가 어디 가시느냐고 물어보았다.

"저, 서당골 윤초시 댁에 가신다. 제사상에라도 놓으시라구……."

"그럼 큰 놈으루 하나 가져가지. 저 얼룩수탉으루……."

이 말에 아버지는 허허 웃고 나서,

"임마, 그래두 이게 실속이 있다."

소년은 공연히 열적어, 책보를 집어던지고는 외양간으로 가, 소 잔등을 한번 철썩 갈겼다. 쇠파리라도 잡는 척.

개울물은 날로 여물어갔다.

소년은 갈림길에서 아래쪽으로 가보았다. 갈밭머리에서 바라보는 서당골 마을은 쪽빛 하늘 아래 한결 가까워 보였다.

어른들의 말이, 내일 소녀네가 양평읍으로 이사 간다는 것이었다. 거기 가서는 조그마한 가겟방을 보게 되리라는 것이었다.

that she was going to move. Really now, there was no reason to feel sorry or sad about it. All the same, the boy paid no attention to the sweet taste of the dates he was eating.

That night the boy went secretly to the place where old grandfather Tok-soe's walnut trees grew. He climbed up in a tree he had spotted during the day, and then began to beat with a stick on a branch he had picked out. The sound of the walnut burrs falling seemed strangely loud. The noise made him tense, afraid of being discovered. Then in the next instant, without knowing just why, he summoned all his strength and beat furiously with the stick, saying, "Come on, big ones, fall! You have to! A lot of you have to fall!"

On the way back home he felt his way carefully, staying in the shadows cast by the three-quarter moon. It was the first time he had ever felt thankful for the shadows.

The boy ran his hands over his bulging pockets. It didn't bother him at all that people say you can get a bad itch from shucking the burrs from walnuts with you bare hands. The walnuts from grandfather Tok-soe's house were supposed to be the best ones in the area, and the boy's only thought

소년은 저도 모르게 주머니 속 호두알을 만지작거리며, 한 손으로는 수없이 갈꽃을 휘어 꺾고 있었다.

그날 밤, 소년은 자리에 누워서도 같은 생각뿐이었다. 내일 소녀네가 이사하는 걸 가보나 어쩌나, 가면 소녀를 보게 될까 어떨까.

그러다가 까무룩 잠이 들었는가 하는데,

"허, 참, 세상 일두……."

마을 갔던 아버지가 언제 돌아왔는지,

"윤초시 댁두 말이 아니여. 그 많던 전답을 다 팔아버리구, 대대루 살아오던 집마저 남의 손에 넘기더니, 또 악상까지 당하는 걸 보면……."

남폿불 밑에서 바느질감을 안고 있던 어머니가,

"증손이라곤 기집애 그 애 하나뿐이었지요?"

"그렇지. 사내애 둘 있던 건 어려서 잃구……."

"어쩌믄 그렇게 자식복이 없을까."

"글쎄 말이지. 이번 앤 꽤 여러 날 앓는 걸 약두 변변히 못 써봤다더군. 지금 같애서는 윤초시네두 대가 끊긴 셈이지. ……그런데 참 이번 기집애는 어린것이 여간 잔망스럽지가 않어. 글쎄 죽기 전에 이런 말을 했다지 않어? 자기가 죽거든 자기 입던 옷을 꼭 그대루 입혀

was that he must get some to the girl right away for her to try.

But then, oh no, he had completely forgotten to ask her to come down to the bank of the stream once more if she got better before they moved away. What a dummy he was. Dummy!

The next day the boy came home from school to find his father dressed in his best clothes, holding a chicken. He asked his father where he was going.

Without responding to the boy's question the father estimated the weight of the chicken he was holding and said, "Suppose this is big enough?"

Bringing out a net bag, his mother said, "You're taking the one that has already cackled several days and is about to start laying. She's not all that big yet, but I guess she's heavy enough."

The boy asked his mother this time where his father was going.

"Oh, he's going to Yun's house over in the schoolhouse valley. It's something for them to put with their sacrifice."

"Then you should send a big one. Like that speckled rooster over there."

The boy's father laughed at this and said, "Come

서 묻어달라구…….”

1) '別로'라는 한자어로 '별나게'의 의미.

* 이 책의 한국어판 저작권은 사단법인 한국문예학술저작권협회로부터 저작물의 사용 허락에 대한 동의를 받았다.

《신문학(新文學)》, 1953

on, son, this one will be fine."

Suddenly the boy felt ashamed. He threw down his schoolbooks and went over to the ox's stall. He gave the ox a slap on the back, making it look as though he was swatting a fly.

Day by day the water in the stream flowed in its course, and the autumn deepened.

The boy went to the fork in the road and looked down the lower way. Beyond the end of the reed fields the village in schoolhouse valley appeared unusually close under the indigo sky.

People in the village had been saying that tomorrow the girl's family would be moving to the town of Yang Pyong. It seemed they planned to try running a little store there.

Unconsciously the boy was fingering the shelled walnuts in his pocket with one hand, and with the other was bending and breaking off reed tassels one after another.

That night as he lay in bed the boy had only one thought on his mind. "Should I go tomorrow and watch when the girl's family is moving? If I go will I get to see the girl? What should I do?"

Then he wasn't quite sure whether he had already been asleep, when he heard, "Huh. Well, that's really strange."

His father, who had been over at the village, had come back.

"And it's really terrible, all that's happened to the Yun family. First they had to sell all their paddies and fields, then they saw the house they've lived in for generations pass into someone else's hands, and now, think of it, on top of all that, they have to suffer this kind of cruel death."

The boy's mother, who sat doing mending in her lap by the light of the lamp, said, "Was that girl the only great-grandchild they had?"

"That's right. The two boys they had died when they were still small."

"I wonder why they've had such bad luck with children in that family?" said his mother.

"I wonder," answered his father. "With this child the sickness lasted a long time, and I hear they couldn't afford to give her the right medicine. The way it is now, the Yun's family line is finished. This girl seems to have been precocious for her age, though. You know, she said that if she died she wanted them to bury her just as she was, right in the clothes she was wearing."

Translated by Edward W. Poitras

해설

Afterword

얼룩진 스웨터

브루스 풀턴

(브리티시 컬럼비아 대학교, 한국문학 및 문학번역, 민영빈 석좌교수)

1952년 10월에 씌어진 단편 「소나기」는 1956년 중앙문화사 발행 소설집 《학》에 실려서 처음 발표되었다. 잡지에는 《신태양》 1959년 4월호에 실린 것이 처음이다. 이 작품은 그 뒤 한국의 국정교과서에 여러 차례 실렸기 때문에 황순원의 작품 중 가장 널리 알려진 것이기도 하다. 그러나 역설적이게도 그같은 우상이 되었기 때문에 단편 양식의 대가로서의 황순원은 제대로 평가를 받지 못하게 되었다. 그가 발표한 백여 편의 단편소설은 한국의 현대 작가들이 쓴 단편소설의 묶음 중에서 가장 세련되고 원숙한 것이라고 말해도 무리가 아닐 듯하다. 그런 작가를 「소나기」라는 단 한 편의 작품으로만

A Stained Sweater

Bruce Fulton (Young-Bin Min Chair in Korean Literature and Literary Translation, University of British Columbia)

"The Cloudburst" (Sonagi 소나기) was written in October 1952, was first anthologized in the story collection *Cranes* (*Hak* 학; Chungang munhwa sa 중앙문화사, 1956), and first appeared in serial form in the April 1959 issue of *New Sun* (Shint'aeyang 신태양). By virtue of being included in numerous editions of Korean public school readers, it is Hwang Sun-Won's best-known story. Ironically its iconic status has hindered recognition of Hwang's mastery of the short story form. The 100-plus works he published in this genre constitute perhaps the most sophisticated and accomplished body of short fiction by a modern Korean writer. But to identify such a writer

아는 것은 노벨상 수상 작가인 어니스트 헤밍웨이를 「깨끗하고 밝은 장소」라는 단편을 통해서만 아는 것과 마찬가지로 별 도움이 안 되는 일이다.

학자들과 평론가들은 황순원을 서정적이고 낭만적이며 미학적인 경향이라고 가정하는 것에 바탕해서 평가하는 경향이 있다. 대다수 독자들은 독자들대로 「소나기」를 어린이들 사이의 순진한 사랑의 이야기로 해석하는 편이다. 그러나 이 작품에는 그런 해석이 암시하는 것 이상의 깊이가 있다. 다른 가능한 여러 가지 해석으로 예컨대 통과의례의 이야기나 탐험의 이야기(소년과 소녀가 함께 가는 산이 그 탐험의 목적지이다)로 볼 수도 있고, 에덴 동산의 이야기와도 유사하게 은총으로부터 타락한 이야기나, 현대(도시에서 온 창백한 피부의 소녀)와 전통(시골에서 자란 가무잡잡한 소년) 간 충돌의 이야기이기도 하다. 혹은 지식과 세련됨을 한 편으로 하고 순진무구함을 다른 한 편으로 한 두 편 사이 대결의 이야기라고도 볼 수 있다.

「소나기」를 통과의례의 이야기라고 보는 해석은 「황순원 작품의 이니시에이션 스토리적 성격」이라는 이재선이 1977년에 발표한 선구적 논문에서 처음으로 제시

with a single story, "The Cloudburst," is no more helpful than to identify, say, the Nobel Prize winning Ernest Hemingway with his story "A Clean, Well-Lighted Place."

Scholars and critics tend to evaluate Hwang Sun-Won on the basis of his presumed lyrical, romantic, and aesthetic tendencies. The great majority of readers for their part tend to interpret "The Cloudburst" as a story of innocent love between children. But the story has much more depth than such a reading suggests. It can be interpreted in a variety of other ways. for example, as an initiation story; a quest (the object of which is represented by the mountain toward which the boy and girl walk on their outing); a Garden of Eden-like fall from grace; a clash between modernity (represented by the pale-skinned girl, who comes from the city) and tradition (represented by the swarthy boy, born and raised in the countryside); or a confrontation between knowledge and sophistication on the one hand, and ignorance and naivete on the other.

The interpretation of "The Cloudburst" as a rite-of-initiation story, first proposed by scholar Yi Chae-sŏn (이재선) in his seminal 1977 essay "Hwang Sun-Won chakp'um ŭi Initiation Story chŏk sŏnggyŏk

되었고, 1996년 하인쯔 인수 펭클이 쓴 「얼룩진 스웨터에 숨겨진 것: 황순원의 '소나기'에 담긴 여성 혐오의 정치학」에서 뒷받침되고 있는데, 꽤 설득력이 있다. 예를 들어서 「소나기」의 끝에서 소녀는 왜 죽는가? 그리고 왜 그 소녀는 죽어가면서 소년과 함께 나들이를 했던 날 입었던 옷을 자신과 함께 묻어달라고 부모에게 부탁하는가? 그 옷의 어떤 면이 그렇게 특별하단 말인가?

소년과 소녀가 함께 나들이 했던 날로부터 며칠 후 다시 만났을 때—나중에 알게 되지만 이것이 그들 사이의 마지막 만남이 된다—소녀가 소년에게 전날 자신이 입었던 분홍 스웨터에 얼룩이 진 것을 보여준다. 그 얼룩은 검붉은 색이고 빠지지 않는다—분명히 핏물이다. 소녀는 그 얼룩이 소년이 자신을 업고 소나기로 불은 강물을 건널 때 소년의 등에서 물들어 생긴 것이라고 믿고 있다.

이처럼 분명한 상징은 해석을 요한다. 소나기를 만나는 시점의 소년과 소녀는 이미 피와 연관된 경험을 한 후이다. 작품의 앞부분에서 소년은 자신이 어리석게 행동하는 것을 몰래 바라보고 있던 소녀를 피하려다 코피를 흘린다. 그리고 그들이 함께 산에 갔을 때 소녀는 칡

(황순원 작품의 Initiation Story적 성격)," and buttressed by writer-scholar-translator Heinz Insu Fenkl's 1996 essay "Buried in a Stained Sweater: The Politics of Misogyny in Hwang Sun-Won's 'Sonagi,'" is persuasive. Why, for example, at the end of "The Cloudburst," does the girl die? And why as she lies dying does she ask her parents to bury her in the clothes she was wearing on the day of her outing with the boy? What is so special about those clothes?

When the boy and girl next meet, several days after their outing—and the last time they see each other, as it turns out—the girl shows the boy a stain on her pink sweater, the same sweater she wore on the day of the outing. The stain is dark red and difficult to remove—apparently a bloodstain. The girl believes the stain came from the boy's back as he carried her piggyback across a stream swollen by rain from the cloudburst.

Such a prominent symbol demands analysis. Already by the time the boy and girl are caught in the cloudburst, each has been associated with blood: earlier in the story the boy has a nosebleed while trying to escape the girl, who has secretly observed him behaving foolishly, and during their outing an arrowroot vine draws blood from the girl's knee.

덩쿨 때문에 무릎에서 피가 나는 경험을 한다. 이어 소나기가 한창 쏟아질 때 소년과 소녀는 비가 새는 원두막을 피해서 수숫단 속에서 비를 피한다. 클라이맥스에 해당하는 이 장면은 강렬한 이미지로 넘친다. 신체 부위를 연상시키는 수숫단의 모양, 수숫단 속으로 들어가기 위해서 그것을 비집어보는 소년의 행동, 소년과 소녀가 웅크리고 들어앉은 수숫단 속의 좁고 어두운 공간, 소년의 등에서 피어오르는 김, 소녀에게 훅 끼쳐오던 소년의 몸냄새.

바로 이런 경험 뒤에 소녀는 병이 나서 죽는다. 그렇다면 우리에게 주어지는 기본적인 이야기는 삶에서 죽음으로 이르는 여행의 이야기이다. 주인공들이 어린이들이므로 이 여행을 통과의례, 성인에 이르는 여행으로 보는 해석에 타당성이 있다. 성인이 되는 일에 따라오는 것은 세상의 경험과 지식, 그리고 궁극적으로는 죽음이다. 소나기는 소년과 소녀가 어린이다운 순진함의 상태에서 어른다운 경험의 상태로 이동하는 것을 상징하는 통과의례의 역할을 한다. 얼룩진 스웨터는 한 영역에서 다른 영역으로 넘어가는 이 통과의 행위를 표시하는 핵심적인 사건의 원형적 상징이다.

And when at the height of the downpour the boy and girl escape the leaky lookout platform they find shelter in a stack of sorghum sheaves. Strong images abound in this climactic scene: the organic shape of the sorghum stack, the boy spreading open the sheaves to inspect it as a place of entry, the tight, dark space inside the stack where the boy and girl huddle, the steam rising from the boy's back, the pungent smell of his body that the girl notices.

It is after this experience that the girl falls ill and dies. We are left, then, with a story that at its most basic is a journey from life to death. Because the protagonists are children it makes sense to view this journey as a coming of age, a journey to adulthood. Adulthood brings with it experience and knowledge of the world, and ultimately death. The cloudburst serves as a symbolic initiation of the boy and girl from a state of innocence and childhood into a state of experience and adulthood. The stained sweater is the archetypal symbol of the core event that marked this passage between the two realms.

"The Cloudburst" is also notable for the characteristic ease with which Hwang Sun-Won shifts

「소나기」에서는 또한 전지적 시점으로부터 제한된 삼인칭 시점으로 자연스럽게 옮아가는 황순원의 솜씨가 눈에 띈다. 그는 이런 전이를 과거시제로부터 현재시제로 이동함으로써 달성한다. 작품의 첫 부분에서 과거시제의 전지적 삼인칭 내러티브를 통해 크게 전경을 그려주는 장면을 주목하라. 그 장면에서는 전지적 시점의 작자가 개울가에서 징검다리 중 하나에 앉아 있는 소녀를 내려다 보고 있다. 그러나 내러티브는 곧 현재시제로 옮아가고, 카메라의 눈은 소년의 눈을 통해서 소녀가 개울로부터 물을 움켜쥐는 모습에 초점을 맞추며 순식간에 그리로 다가간다.

주제와 내러티브 양식은 황순원의 여러 강점 중 두 가지에 지나지 않는다. 그는 현대 한국 소설가들 중 어느 누구 못지 않게 세련된 이야기꾼이기도 하며, 인간의 심리와 정신에 대한 그의 통찰력과 유연하고 열린 그의 세계관은 그를 시공을 초월한 보편적인 단편소설가로 만들어준다. 방언의 구사, 시골과 도시라는 배경 모두를 다루는 숙련된 솜씨, 다양한 내러티브의 기술, 생생한 예술적 상상력, 다양한 인물군, 그리고 인간 성격에 대한 통찰로 인해서 황순원은 모든 것을 갖춘 작

from omniscient to limited third-person point of view. This he accomplishes by shifting from past tense to present tense. Notice at the beginning of the story the scene outlined in panorama through past-tense omniscient third-person narrative: the boy on the bank of the stream peering down at the girl perched on one of the stepping stones that cross the stream. But soon the narrative shifts to present tense and the author's camera eye zooms in to focus, through the eyes of the boy, on what the girl is doing as she scoops water from the stream.

Theme and narrative style are but two of Hwang's strong suits. He is also as polished a storyteller as any fiction writer of modern Korea, and his insights into the human heart and mind and his flexible and open-ended world view make him a short-story writer for the ages. Indeed it is his craftsmanship that sets Hwang apart from his peers. His command of dialect, his facility with both rural and urban settings, his variety of narrative techniques, his vivid artistic imagination, his diverse constellation of characters, and his insights into human personality make Hwang at once a complete writer and one who is almost impossible to categorize. Modern Korea has produced a number of short story masters, but

가이자 어떤 한 카테고리로 묶기가 거의 불가능한 작가이기도 하다. 현대 한국에서는 단편소설의 거장이 상당수 배출되었으나 황순원은 그중에서도 가장 탁월하다. 거기에는 여러 가지 이유가 있다.

첫째로 황순원은 현대 한국의 가장 위대한 이야기꾼 중의 한 사람이다. 둘째로 그의 한국어 구사력은 선망의 대상이다. 단어를 낭비하는 법이 없고 내러티브의 리듬이나 대구를 위해서가 아니라면 같은 말을 반복하는 일도 없다. 황순원의 한국어 구사력과 정치한 문체로 인해서 그의 작품을 영어로 번역하는 일도 더 용이해진다. 그가 백여 편이 넘는 다양한 단편을 썼다는 사실도 매력적이다. 그중에는 자연주의적인 작품에서 초현실주의적인 작품까지 온갖 경향의 작품이 다 있다. 배경은 시골이기도 하고 도시이기도 하며, 산이기도 하고 바닷가이기도 하고, 때로는 구체적인 한국이 배경이지만 특히 초기작들에서는 보편적인 배경이 자주 등장하는 편이다. 어떤 작품들은 자전적이지만 대부분은 삼인칭을 사용하고 있다. 그의 주인공은 어린이에서 노인, 동물까지, 유식한 사람에서 무지한 사람에 이르기까지 다양하다. 황순원은 지역적 관습과 방언을 존중하

Hwang stands above them all. There are a number of reasons for this.

First of all, Hwang is one of the great storytellers of modern Korea. Second, his command of the Korean language is enviable. He wastes few words and, except when he uses repetition to establish a narrative rhythm or parallelism, rarely repeats himself. Not surprisingly, Hwang's mastery of Korean and his precision of style make his stories more amenable to English translation. Also appealing is the great variety of Hwang's hundred-plus stories. They range from the naturalistic to the surreal. Their settings are rural or urban, mountain or seaside, sometimes specifically Korean and, more often in his early stories, sometimes culturally nonspecific. Some stories are autobiographical, but the majority are told in the third person. His protagonists range from children to the elderly to animals, from the educated to the uneducated. Hwang is attentive to local customs and dialect and knowledgeable about Korean folklore.

Hwang Sun-Won is the Korean short-fiction writer of transcendence. He was solidly rooted in Korean tradition but instead of being bound by it was able to incorporate that tradition into a broader creative

고 한국 민담에 대해 잘 알고 있다.

황순원은 한국의 탁월한 단편 작가이다. 한국적 전통에 단단히 뿌리박고 있으면서도 거기 구애되지 않으며, 예술적 상상력을 발휘해서 긴 창작의 일생 동안 지속적으로 발전시켜온 넓은 창조적 비전에 그 전통을 통합시키기도 한다. 황순원은 한국 단편소설을 다른 어느 현대 소설가들보다도 더욱 높이 세계 무대로 끌어올린 작가이다.

vision, such that his artistic imagination continued to develop throughout his long career. More than any other modern Korean fiction writer it is Hwang who elevated the Korean short story to the world stage.

비평의 목소리

Critical Acclaim

황순원 문학은 모든 곳에 살고 있는 모든 사람들과 관련된 문제들—무엇보다도 인간의 고독, 시간의 흐름, 순진함의 상실, 그리고 남녀간의 불안정한 거리 등—을 다룬다. 존재에 따르는 이러한 본질적인 문제들에 대해 절망한 작가들도 있지만 황순원의 작품에는 희망과 결의와 의미를 암시하는 강력한 도덕적 기반이 있다. 황순원은 종종 외롭고 고립된 인물들을 그리지만 그들의 삶에 대한 그의 초점은 궁극적으로는 그들이 가끔씩 경험하는 암울한 공허로부터 그들이 순간적으로 느끼는 연결이 지닌 절묘한 성격으로 이동한다.

마틴 홀먼, "「소나기」: 서문," 마틴 홀먼 편,

Hwang's literature takes up questions that touch all people everywhere: among others, human loneliness and the passage of time, the loss of innocence, and the uneasy distance between men and women. While these inherent problems of existence have led some writers to despair, there is a strong moral underpinning to Hwang's work that suggests hope, resolution, and meaning. Hwang often portrays characters who are lonely and isolated, but ultimately he shifts his focus on their lives from the bleak emptiness they often experience to the exquisite nature of their moments of juncture."

Martin Holman, "소나기": "Introduction," *The Book of Masks:*

『가면들의 책: 황순원 단편선』(런던: 리더스 인터내셔널, 1989)

그의 문장들은 정치하고 섬세하게 구축되어 있다. 모든 요소에는 역할이 있고 모든 단어는 제 위치에 있는 것으로 보이며 단어와 구절의 관계는 항상 분명하다. (……) 황순원은 우리가 알아야 할 것만을 우리가 알아야 할 때에만 얘기해 준다. 그는 풍경을 그리거나 꽃이나 벌레와 한가하게 놀고 있지 않다. 그는 기본적으로 인간 세계의 아름다움과 인간 감정의 표현에 관심이 있다. 그리고 시사적인 문맥에서 섬세한 세부를 통해 그 점을 드러낸다. 그 결과 황순원 이야기의 세계는 우리가 일상에서 벗어나 그 세계에 살고 있는 사람들과 공명하는 한에서만 우리에게 드러난다. 우리는 거의 항상 황순원이 우리에게 이야기해 주는 것 이상의 무엇이 있을 것이라고 느끼게 된다. 우리는 빛의 바로 너머에 있는 어두움과 신비를 감지한다.

마샬 필, "「소나기」: 한 이야기의 해부," 『세계와 나』

1990년 3월, 375, 378

Stories by Hwang Sun-Won, ed. Martin Holman

(London: Readers International, 1989)

His sentences are tightly and carefully packed: Every element has its task, each word seems in its proper place, and the relationships between words and phrases are always clear. [...] Hwang tells us only what we need to know and only when we need to know it. He does not paint landscapes or dally with flowers or insects; he is primarily concerned with the beauty of the human world and the expression of human feeling. And this he reveals with careful detail in telling contexts. As a result, the world of a Hwang Sun-Won story is removed from our daily world and is revealed to us only insofar as it resonates with the people who populate it. Nearly always we feel there is more out there than what Hwang is telling us; we sense darkness and mystery just beyond the light.

Marshall R. Pihl, "소나기": "Anatomy of a Story,"

The World & I, March 1990, pp. 375, 378

His agitated, yet potentially powerful, conscious-

의식의 흔들림과 잠재력은 이후 전쟁 체험 등의 역사적 관련과 순정한 문학의 본령에 대한 집요함에 근거하여 직결정치한 구조력과 서정성 및 상징의 음영으로 결정되는 「학」「소나기」 등 100여 편의 단편소설을 생산하게 된다. 뿐만 아니라 50년대 이후 장편으로 발전, 『카인의 후예』『나무들 비탈에 서다』에서 이념적인 분극화 과정이 일으킨 격동과 6·25 전쟁에 의해 빚어진 비탈진 현실의 갈등과 상황적인 모순에 얽힌 한국인들의 삶의 훼손과 고뇌 및 그 극복의 문제를 형상화하고.(……)

이재선, 『현대 한국소설사: 1945-1990』 민음사, 1991

그의 소설은 대상의 사실적인 인식보다 묘사의 집중력과 특유의 서정성을 바탕으로 한 정서적 감응력이 중시된다. 그의 단편소설을 평가하는 데에 관형적으로 붙는 "서정적"이라는 용어는 작품의 주제나 격조를 가리키는 말이다. 그리고 이것은 그가 활용하고 있는 작품 구조의 개방적 결말 형식, 응축된 문장과 감각적인 언어를 통해 실현되는 전체적인 분위기와도 연관된다. 황순원의 단편소설에서 즐겨 구사했던 간결한 문장 호흡과 감각적인 언어가 환기하는 정서가 인상적이다.

ness carried him through his later war experiences and led to his persistent efforts to achieve a truly pure literature, with more than a hundred short stories characterized by intricate plots, lyricism, and nuanced symbols, including "Crane" and "Cloudburst." In addition, he expanded his scope in the 1950s and depicted damaged and anguished Korean lives intertwined with post-liberation and post-war ideological conflicts and situational contradictions, as well as the Korean people's efforts to overcome these issues, in novels like *The Descendants of Cain* and *Trees on a Slope*.

Lee Jae-seon, *History of Modern Korean Fiction: 1945-1990*

(Seoul: Minum, 1991)

In his fiction, emotional sensitivity, revealed in the intensity of his depictions and his trademark lyricism, are much more important than factual recognition of objects. A common adjective used to describe his short stories, "lyrical," points to their theme and style. This quality is also related to the open-ended endings of his stories and their overall atmosphere, created through his use of a sensuous vocabulary. The emotional effect that Hwang's

권영민, 「소나기」, 『한국현대문학사』, 제 2권, 1945-2000,

민음사, 2002, 119쪽

trademark short sentences and sensuous vocabulary evoke is impressive.

Kwon Yeong-min, *History of Modern Korean Literature: 1945-2000* (Seoul: Minum, 2002), 119

황순원

황순원은 오늘날의 북한 지역 평양 근처에서 1915년에 태어나서 교육을 받았으며 도쿄의 와세다 대학에서 공부하던 기간 동안 세계 문학을 두루 섭렵했다. 20대에 갓 들어섰을 때 두 권의 시집을 냈고 1940년에 첫 창작집을 상재했다. 그 이후에는 소설에 몰두해서 7편의 장편과 100여 편이 넘는 단편을 발표했다. 말년에 시로 돌아가서 1992년에 출간된 그의 마지막 작품은 시집이었다. 2000년에 사망했다.

1946년 소련 점령하의 북한 지역에서 급진적인 토지개혁이 진행되고 있는—이 일은 그가 1954년에 발표한 소설『카인의 후예』의 배경이 되었다—가운데 지주 집안 출신인 황순원은 부모와 아내, 자식들과 함께 미군 점령하의 남한으로 갔다. 그해 9월부터 서울고등학교에서 교사로 학생들을 가르치기 시작했다. 수백만의 다른 한국인들처럼 황순원의 가족도 1950년에서 1953년에 이르는 내전 기간 동안 피난생활을 했다. 전후에 서울로 돌아가 교사 생활을 계속하다가 1957년에서 1993

Hwang Sun-Won

Hwang Sun-Won was born in 1915 near Pyongyang in present-day North Korea and was educated there and at Waseda University in Tokyo, where he read widely in world literature. He was barely in his twenties when he produced two volumes of poetry, and in 1940 his first volume of stories was published. He subsequently concentrated on fiction, turning out seven novels and more than one hundred stories. In his later years he came full circle: his last published works (1992) were poems. He died in 2000.

In 1946 in the midst of the radical land reform instituted in the Soviet-occupied northern sector of Korea—the backdrop for his 1954 novel *The Descendants of Cain* (K'ain ŭi huye 카인의 후예), Hwang, a member of a landed family, left with his parents, wife, and children for the American-occupied South. There, in September of that year, he began teaching at Seoul High School. Like millions of other Koreans, the Hwang family was displaced by the civil war of 1950-53. Returning to Seoul, Hwang

년까지 경희대학교에서 문예창작을 가르쳤다.

황순원의 몇몇 작품들은 현대 한국에서 가장 널리 알려진 작품들로, 「별」(1940), 「황노인」(1942), 「독 짓는 늙은이」(1944), 「학」(1953), 「목넘이 마을의 개」(1948) 등이 그것이다. 1950년대 중반 왕성한 창작열로 수많은 단편을 써서 1958년 『잃어버린 사람들』이라는 단편집으로 묶어 출판했다. 이 책은 고도로 구조화된 사회에서의 국외자라는 주제에 대한 일련의 변주로 이루어져 있으며 그 주제의 일관성으로 인해서 황순원의 단편집 중에서 독특한 존재이다.

1950년대에는 장편도 여러 편 발표했으며 그 이후 20여 년 동안 주요 장편들을 발표했다. 『나무들 비탈에 서다』(1960)는 세 명의 젊은 군인에게 한국전쟁이 미친 영향을 다룬 작품으로 아마도 그의 가장 성공적인 장편이라 할 수 있다. 『일월』(1968)은 자신이 백정이라는 천민계급에 속한다는 사실을 뒤늦게 깨달으며 그 사실과 화해하는 젊은 지식인의 초상이다. 1972년 발표한 『움직이는 성』은 현대 한국에서 서양의 영향과 고유의 전통을 종합하려 한 야심 찬 시도의 작품이다.

1960년대와 1970년대는 황순원의 작품들 중 가장 실

resumed teaching, and from 1957 to 1993 he taught creative writing at Kyunghee University (경희대학교).

Hwang is the author of some of the best-known stories of modern Korea: "The Stars" (Pyŏl 별, 1940); "Old Man Hwang" (Hwang noin 황노인, 1942); "The Old Potter" (Tok chinnŭn nŭlgŭni 독지는 늙어니, 1944); "Cranes" (Hak 학, 1953); and "The Dog of Crossover Village" (Mongnŏmi maul ŭi kae 목넘이 마을의 개, 1948). In a creative burst in the mid-1950s he produced the stories published collectively in 1958 as *Lost Souls* (Irŏbŏrin saram tŭl 잃어버린 사람들). This volume, a series of variations on the theme of the outcast in a highly structured society, is distinctive among Hwang's story collections for its thematic unity.

Also in the 1950s Hwang began publishing novels. During the next two decades he produced his most important work in this genre. *Trees on a Slope* (Namu tŭl pit'al e soda 나무들 비탈에 서다, 1960), perhaps his most successful novel, deals with the effects of the civil war on three young soldiers. *The Sun and the Moon* (Irwŏl 일월, 1968) is a portrait of a young intellectual coming to terms with the belated realization that he is a *paekchŏng* (백정 outcaste). *The Moving Fortress* (Umjiginŭn song 움직이는 성, 1972) is an ambitious effort to synthesize Western influence and na-

험적인 단편이 쓰인 시기이기도 하다. 가장 기억에 남는 그의 단편들 중 일부가 이 시기에 쓰였으니,「어머니가 있는 유월의 대화」(1965),「막은 내렸는데」(1968),「숫자풀이」(1974) 등이 그것이다. 황순원의 창작력은 1980년대에도 줄어들지 않아서 무척 독창적인 작품인「그림자 풀이」(1984)는 그 점을 증명하는 좋은 예이다.

작가로서의 황순원은 완벽주의자였다. 그는 규칙적인 창작 스케줄을 유지했고, 한 번에 한 편의 작품에 집중해서 여러 차례 개고를 거쳐 출판했다. 그는 또한 이후 판본을 낼 때 이미 출간된 작품들을 다시 개고한 것으로도 잘 알려져 있다. 한국인들이 한국어로 작품을 발표하는 것이 거의 불가능하던 일제하 암흑기에는 자신의 시골집에 친구들을 모아 자신이 쓴 작품들을 낭독하곤 했다. 아마도 이런 습관이 그의 작품에 나오는 대화에서 완벽한 가락이 느껴지는 이유일 것이다.

작가로서 황순원이 지킨 엄격성은 그의 독자에 대한 존중에서도 나타난다. 그의 열린 결말은 독자들이 원하는 대로 읽고 해석하는 것을 허락한다. 그는 독자들에게 무거운 메시지를 강요하지 않았다.

황순원은 대대로 기독교인 집안에서 자라났지만 그

tive tradition in modern Korea.

Also in the 1960s and 1970s Hwang's short fiction became more experimental. Some of his most memorable and challenging stories date from this period: "Conversation in June about Mothers" (Ŏmŏni ka innŭn yuwŏl ŭi taehwa 어머니 가 있는 유월의 대화, 1965), "The Curtain Fell, But Then..." (Mag ûn naeryŏnnŭnde 막은 내렸는데, 1968), "A Numerical Enigma" (Sutcha p'uri 수자풀이, 1974). Hwang's creative powers were undiminished as late as the 1980s, as the highly original "A Shadow Solution" (Kŭrimja p'uri 그림자 풀이, 1984) demonstrates.

As a writer, Hwang was a perfectionist. He observed a regular writing schedule, working on one story at a time and then revising and editing before first publication. He was also known to revise published versions of his stories for subsequent editions. During the late years of the Japanese occupation (암흑기), when it was virtually impossible for Koreans to publish in their own language, Hwang would gather his friends at his rural home and read aloud to them drafts of his stories—a practice that may help account for the pitch-perfect dialogue of many of his stories.

His integrity as a writer is also seen in his respect

의 조상들 중에는 정통 주자학자도 있다. 개인적으로는 감정이입을 잘하고 호기심이 많으며 상대방을 존중하는 사람이었다. 그는 모든 사람에게서, 그리고 모든 생물에게서 존엄성을 보았다. 그의 작품 중 많은 작품들이 어린이와 동물, 그리고 사회의 주변인들을 다루고 있다. 어린 시절 어른들의 발치에서 많은 이야기를 듣고 자람으로써 거장 이야기꾼이 되었다. 탁월한 유머감각의 소유자였으며 독주를 즐겼고 (그가 가장 좋아하던 술은 쌀로 만든 고도로 정제된 술인 법주였다) 말할 때는 듣기 좋은 평안도 사투리를 사용했다. 작가로서뿐만 아니라 개인으로서도 탁월한 인물이었다.

for readers. His open-ended works allow them to read and interpret as they saw fit. He does not hammer them over the head with weighty messages.

Hwang Sun-Won came from a multi-generation Christian family, but also counted among his ancestors a neo-Confucian gentleman noted for his orthodox ways. In person he was empathic, curious, and respectful; he saw dignity in every person, indeed every living creature. Many of his works deal with children, animals, and those on the margins of society. He was a master storyteller, having heard many a story at the feet of his elders during his childhood. He had a terrific sense of humor, enjoyed brew and spirits (his favorite was *pŏpchu* 법주, a highly refined rice brew), and spoke with a delightful P'yŏngan Province accent. He was outstanding as a person as well as a writer.

번역 **에드워드 포이트라스** Translated by Edward W. Poitras

에드워드 포이트라스는 1970년대부터 한국의 소설, 시, 학술 저작물 등을 번역하였다. 한국에서 번역상을 수상했으며, 또한 직접 한국어로 저술한 저작물에 대한 상도 수상한 바 있다. 현재 현역 활동에서 은퇴한 뒤 미국 미네소타에서 번역가인 아내 즈넬과 살고 있다.

Edward W. Poitras has been publishing translations of Korean fiction, poetry and academic writings since the 1970's. He has won awards for his translations and also for his original works in Korean. He is now retired and living with his wife Genell, also a translator, in Minnesota in the United States.

바이링궐 에디션 한국 대표 소설 106

소나기

2015년 1월 9일 초판 1쇄 발행

지은이 황순원 | **옮긴이** 에드워드 포이트라스 | **펴낸이** 김재범
기획위원 정은경, 전성태, 이경재 | **편집** 정수인, 이은혜, 김형욱, 윤단비 | **관리** 박신영
펴낸곳 (주)아시아 | **출판등록** 2006년 1월 27일 제406-2006-000004호
주소 서울특별시 동작구 서달로 161-1(흑석동 100-16)
전화 02.821.5055 | **팩스** 02.821.5057 | **홈페이지** www.bookasia.org
ISBN 979-11-5662-067-9 (set) | 979-11-5662-083-9 (04810)
값은 뒤표지에 있습니다.

Bi-lingual Edition Modern Korean Literature 106

The Cloudburst

Written by Hwang Sun-Won I **Translated by** Edward W. Poitras
Published by Asia Publishers I 161-1, Seodal-ro, Dongjak-gu, Seoul, Korea
Homepage Address www.bookasia.org I **Tel**. (822).821.5055 I **Fax**. (822).821.5057
First published in Korea by Asia Publishers 2015
ISBN 979-11-5662-067-9 (set) | 979-11-5662-083-9 (04810)

바이링궐 에디션 한국 대표 소설

한국문학의 가장 중요하고 첨예한 문제의식을 가진 작가들의 대표작을 주제별로 선정!
하버드 한국학 연구원 및 세계 각국의 한국문학 전문 번역진이 참여한 번역 시리즈!
미국 하버드대학교와 컬럼비아대학교 동아시아학과, 캐나다 브리티시컬럼비아대학교 아시아학과 등 해외 대학에서 교재로 채택!

바이링궐 에디션 한국 대표 소설 set 1

분단 Division

01 병신과 머저리-**이청준** The Wounded-**Yi Cheong-jun**
02 어둠의 혼-**김원일** Soul of Darkness-**Kim Won-il**
03 순이삼촌-**현기영** Sun-i Samch'on-**Hyun Ki-young**
04 엄마의 말뚝 1-**박완서** Mother's Stake I-**Park Wan-suh**
05 유형의 땅-**조정래** The Land of the Banished-**Jo Jung-rae**

산업화 Industrialization

06 무진기행-**김승옥** Record of a Journey to Mujin-**Kim Seung-ok**
07 삼포 가는 길-**황석영** The Road to Sampo-**Hwang Sok-yong**
08 아홉 켤레의 구두로 남은 사내-**윤흥길** The Man Who Was Left as Nine Pairs of Shoes-**Yun Heung-gil**
09 돌아온 우리의 친구-**신상웅** Our Friend's Homecoming-**Shin Sang-ung**
10 원미동 시인-**양귀자** The Poet of Wŏnmi-dong-**Yang Kwi-ja**

여성 Women

11 중국인 거리-**오정희** Chinatown-**Oh Jung-hee**
12 풍금이 있던 자리-**신경숙** The Place Where the Harmonium Was-**Shin Kyung-sook**
13 하나코는 없다-**최윤** The Last of Hanak'o-**Ch'oe Yun**
14 인간에 대한 예의-**공지영** Human Decency-**Gong Ji-young**
15 빈처-**은희경** Poor Man's Wife-**Eun Hee-kyung**

바이링궐 에디션 한국 대표 소설 set 2

자유 Liberty

16 필론의 돼지-**이문열** Pilon's Pig-**Yi Mun-yol**
17 슬로우 불릿-**이대환** Slow Bullet-**Lee Dae-hwan**
18 직선과 독가스-**임철우** Straight Lines and Poison Gas-**Lim Chul-woo**
19 깃발-**홍희담** The Flag-**Hong Hee-dam**
20 새벽 출정-**방현석** Off to Battle at Dawn-**Bang Hyeon-seok**

사랑과 연애 Love and Love Affairs

21 별을 사랑하는 마음으로-**윤후명** With the Love for the Stars-**Yun Hu-myong**
22 목련공원-**이승우** Magnolia Park-**Lee Seung-u**
23 칼에 찔린 자국-**김인숙** Stab-**Kim In-suk**
24 회복하는 인간-**한강** Convalescence-**Han Kang**
25 트렁크-**정이현** In the Trunk-**Jeong Yi-hyun**

남과 북 South and North

26 판문점-**이호철** Panmunjom-**Yi Ho-chol**
27 수난 이대-**하근찬** The Suffering of Two Generations-**Ha Geun-chan**
28 분지-**남정현** Land of Excrement-**Nam Jung-hyun**
29 봄 실상사-**정도상** Spring at Silsangsa Temple-**Jeong Do-sang**
30 은행나무 사랑-**김하기** Gingko Love-**Kim Ha-kee**

바이링궐 에디션 한국 대표 소설 set 3

서울 Seoul

31 눈사람 속의 검은 항아리-**김소진** The Dark Jar within the Snowman-**Kim So-jin**
32 오후, 가로지르다-**하성란** Traversing Afternoon-**Ha Seong-nan**
33 나는 봉천동에 산다-**조경란** I Live in Bongcheon-dong-**Jo Kyung-ran**
34 그렇습니까? 기린입니다-**박민규** Is That So? I'm A Giraffe-**Park Min-gyu**
35 성탄특선-**김애란** Christmas Specials-**Kim Ae-ran**

전통 Tradition

36 무자년의 가을 사흘-**서정인** Three Days of Autumn, 1948-**Su Jung-in**
37 유자소전-**이문구** A Brief Biography of Yuja-**Yi Mun-gu**
38 향기로운 우물 이야기-**박범신** The Fragrant Well-**Park Bum-shin**
39 월행-**송기원** A Journey under the Moonlight-**Song Ki-won**
40 협죽도 그늘 아래-**성석제** In the Shade of the Oleander-**Song Sok-ze**

아방가르드 Avant-garde

41 아겔다마-**박상륭** Akeldama-**Park Sang-ryoong**
42 내 영혼의 우물-**최인석** A Well in My Soul-**Choi In-seok**
43 당신에 대해서-**이인성** On You-**Yi In-seong**
44 회색 時-**배수아** Time In Gray-**Bae Su-ah**
45 브라운 부인-**정영문** Mrs. Brown-**Jung Young-moon**

바이링궐 에디션 한국 대표 소설 set 4

디아스포라 Diaspora

46 속옷-**김남일** Underwear-Kim Nam-il
47 상하이에 두고 온 사람들-**공선옥** People I Left in Shanghai-Gong Sun-ok
48 모두에게 복된 새해-**김연수** Happy New Year to Everyone-Kim Yeon-su
49 코끼리-**김재영** The Elephant-Kim Jae-young
50 먼지별-**이경** Dust Star-Lee Kyung

가족 Family

51 혜자의 눈꽃-**천승세** Hye-ja's Snow-Flowers-Chun Seung-sei
52 아베의 가족-**전상국** Ahbe's Family-Jeon Sang-guk
53 문 앞에서-**이동하** Outside the Door-Lee Dong-ha
54 그리고, 축제-**이혜경** And Then the Festival-Lee Hye-kyung
55 봄밤-**권여선** Spring Night-Kwon Yeo-sun

유머 Humor

56 오늘의 운세-**한창훈** Today's Fortune-Han Chang-hoon
57 새-**전성태** Bird-Jeon Sung-tae
58 밀수록 다시 가까워지는-**이기호** So Far, and Yet So Near-Lee Ki-ho
59 유리방패-**김중혁** The Glass Shield-Kim Jung-hyuk
60 전당포를 찾아서-**김종광** The Pawnshop Chase-Kim Chong-kwang

바이링궐 에디션 한국 대표 소설 set 5

관계 Relationship

61 도둑견습 – **김주영** Robbery Training-Kim Joo-young
62 사랑하라, 희망 없이 – **윤영수** Love, Hopelessly-Yun Young-su
63 봄날 오후, 과부 셋 – **정지아** Spring Afternoon, Three Widows-Jeong Ji-a
64 유턴 지점에 보물지도를 묻다 - **윤성희** Burying a Treasure Map at the U-turn-Yoon Sung-hee
65 쀼이거나 쯰이거나 - **백가흠** Puy, Thuy, Whatever-Paik Ga-huim

일상의 발견 Discovering Everyday Life

66 나는 음식이다 – **오수연** I Am Food-Oh Soo-yeon
67 트럭 – **강영숙** Truck-Kang Young-sook
68 통조림 공장 - **편혜영** The Canning Factory-Pyun Hye-young
69 꽃 – **부희령** Flowers-Pu Hee-ryoung
70 피의일요일 – **윤이형** BloodySunday-Yun I-hyeong

금기와 욕망 Taboo and Desire

71 북소리 - **송영** Drumbeat-**Song Yong**
72 발칸의 장미를 내게 주었네 - **정미경** He Gave Me Roses of the Balkans-**Jung Mi-kyung**
73 아무도 돌아오지 않는 밤 – **김숨** The Night Nobody Returns Home-**Kim Soom**
74 젓가락여자 – **천운영** Chopstick Woman-**Cheon Un-yeong**
75 아직 일어나지 않은 일 – **김미월** What Has Yet to Happen-**Kim Mi-wol**

바이링궐 에디션 한국 대표 소설 set 6

운명 Fate

76 언니를 놓치다 – **이경자** Losing a Sister-Lee Kyung-ja
77 아들 – **윤정모** Father and Son-Yoon Jung-mo
78 명두 – **구효서** Relics-Ku Hyo-seo
79 모독 – **조세희** Insult-Cho Se-hui
80 화요일의 강 – **손홍규** Tuesday River-Son Hong-gyu

미의 사제들 Aesthetic Priests

81 고수 – **이외수** Grand Master-Lee Oisoo
82 말을 찾아서 – **이순원** Looking for a Horse-Lee Soon-won
83 상춘곡 – **윤대녕** Song of Everlasting Spring-Youn Dae-nyeong
84 삭매와 자미 – **김별아** Sakmae and Jami-Kim Byeol-ah
85 저만치 혼자서 – **김훈** Alone Over There-Kim Hoon

식민지의 벌거벗은 자들 The Naked in the Colony

86 감자 – **김동인** Potatoes-Kim Tong-in
87 운수 좋은 날 – **현진건** A Lucky Day-Hyŏn Chin'gŏn
88 탈출기 – **최서해** Escape-Ch'oe So-hae
89 과도기 – **한설야** Transition-Han Seol-ya
90 지하촌 – **강경애** The Underground Village-Kang Kyŏng-ae